Authors

Brian Gilan

Matt Ganderson

Dedications

To my two nonexistent children: for not distracting me and allowing me to sleep.

To my two master's degrees unrelated to writing: thanks for nothing, other than student loan debt.

ISBN: 9781794493766

Lenny was a normal boy with normal skills.

While Lenny loved lemonade,

His mom loved martinis and pills.

His dad loved business and dollar bills.

2

Lenny and his friends dreamt of changing the world.

One of Lenny's dreams that never seemed to fade

Was giving the world free lemonade.

4

With passion he normally only showed his secretary,
Lenny's dad put him on a profit mission.

Lenny was later visited by the profit fairy,
And earned nocturnal commission.

Lenny launched out of bed excited and erect.

At school recess he launched a lemonade stand
With his best friend Noah on hand.

Noah
Co-founder 1b

Lenny
Co-founder 1a

D.A.R.E.

TO RESIST
PUBERTY
AND ACNE

DON'T FALL

Imaginary Sloth Friend
Head of Anxiety

They created The **F-U-N Mission Statement** that day
To guide how they would play.

They pitched their business idea to Lenny's mom under discretion. Her purse was the only available capital after the **last recess session.**

The boys started with a **Limited Lemon Release**,
And watched the line steadily increase.

Proving product-market fit:
The lemonade stand was a hit!

With early cash in hand,
Lenny expanded his team to meet demand.

Shane - Sales
- Sporty
- Cool
- Mediocre at school

Albert – Accounting & Finance
- Mathlete
- Geek
- Would rather not speak

Diversity

Jill - Marketing
- Creative
- Good with adversity
- Checks box on diversity

They had a team offsite,
And were forced to say nice things and not fight.

They memorized The F-U-N Mission Statement way.
Lenny **CULT**ivated a company **CULT**ure that day.

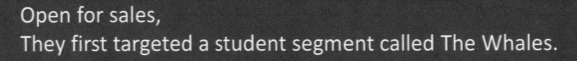

Open for sales,
They first targeted a student segment called The Whales.

THE WHITE WHALES

White children of wealthy lawyers and doctors with discretionary coins to spend on high-end sugary sweets.

1% of playground population.

TRAITS:
- Entitled
- Elitist
- Low Price Sensitivity

They eventually **penetrated** the entire playground at recess.
The lemonade stand was officially a sweet su¢¢e$$!

Lenny's piggy bank grew with each sold drink.
He bought new toys
To change how the **cool kids** think.

Lenny's dad had never been so **proud**.
His son was a business boy,
And finally fit in with the crowd.

As Lenny stood tall,
Seasons suddenly shifted from Summer to Fall.

With recess indoors, there were no profits to gain,
And a pivot to hot chocolate didn't cure the pain.
Girl Scout cookies depleted the chocolate supply chain.

This left quality in question.
Seasonality caused **The Great Recess Recession.**

Days passed without earning a cent.
At a sleepover, Lenny's dad joined as an emergency chaperone,
And forced Lenny to fire the bottom 60 percent.

This included Jill who was scheduled for "maturity leave".
Only Shane from Sales stayed,
Because he knew how to make decision-makers believe.

Noah threw a pity party for all to see,
And filed a copycat complaint,
Claiming Lenny stole his lemonade recipe.

Noah won a lump sum pudding snack settlement.
Lenny filed for Chapter 11,
Going beyond his reading level and funding spent.

Lenny's **life was lacking** after lemonade.

As his lonely mind wandered and twisted,
Lenny's dad and the cool kids forgot Lenny existed.

Lenny asked his dad for career advice, to which he replied,

Forget your values,
And let money be your guide.

Lenny rode his bicycle to clear his mind.

Eventually deciding to give in to the grind.

Driven by his dad's criteria,
He began working in the school cafeteria.

Inspired by a fresh new start,
Lenny tried to figure out the org chart.

He quickly found it was top-down culture
Led by Principal Howzit: a dream-crushing vulture.

Principal Howzit

VP Pizza VP Fries VP Juice VP Trash

Lunch Lady Middle Management Janitors

Everyone always said "**Yes**" to Principal Howzit to win.
Lenny found this culture silly, but learned to fit in.

Lenny first sold **orange juice** aligned with his interests.
After a reorganization he sold **Brussels sprouts** and indifference.

Lenny found a healthy segment from a playground poll,
And made Semester 2 Principal's Club after crushing his sales goal.

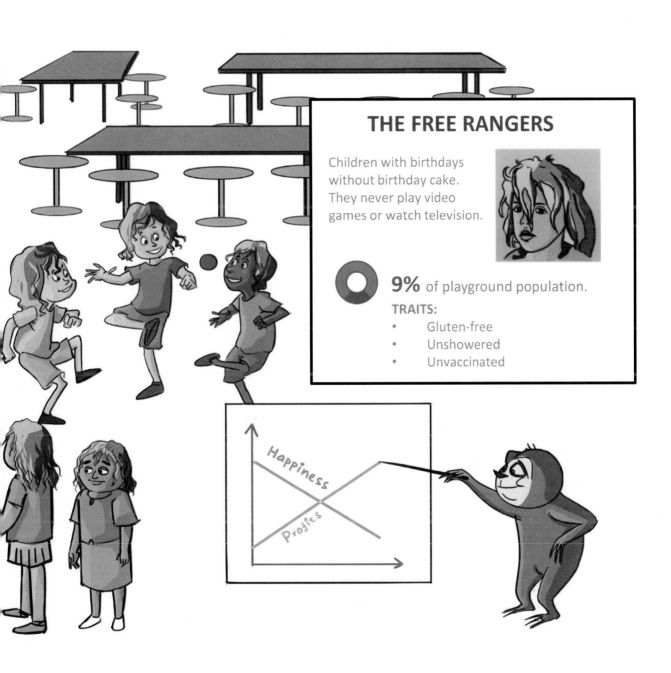

THE FREE RANGERS

Children with birthdays without birthday cake. They never play video games or watch television.

9% of playground population.

TRAITS:
- Gluten-free
- Unshowered
- Unvaccinated

He spent time preparing for **meetings**
About other **meetings**
His manager spoke in buzzwords and awkward greetings.

These words buzzed over his head.
He blocked time on his calendar to get ahead,
But people scheduled **meetings** over his blocked time instead.

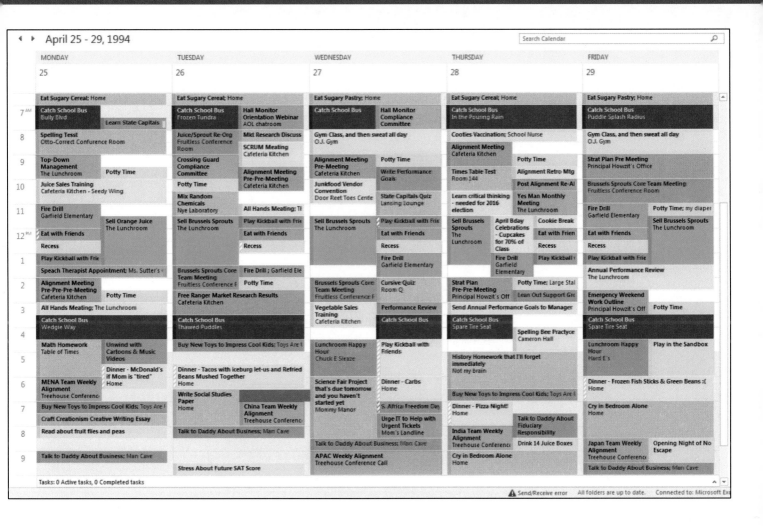

Action Items
- Make Lenny feel self-conscious
- Give Lenny anxiety on Sunday nights
- Inform Lenny he's not good enough

He even had calls at night instead of playing with toys.
It was impossible to hear with all the background noise.

Lenny almost called it quits,
But was too attached to benefits:
1. Annual extra credits
2. Book report edits
3. Pizza and fries in excess
4. Unlimited recess[1]

[1] no time to actually take recess

Back at work, he tried to avoid gossip
During each drinking fountain trip.

With no place
For white space,

Sometimes Lenny sat alone in the handicap bathroom stall,
Swiping through cooties just to get away from it all.

Lenny had many projects with no time to delay,
But **fire drills** often got in the way.

While there was no time to plan or discuss,
He spent plenty of time thrown under the school bus.

Lenny's performance was graded worse than his report card.
While Lenny's coworker, Ramona, starred.

She was a master of spin.
While Lenny was **stressing out**, Ramona was **leaning in**.

Lenny worked nights so he didn't fall behind.
He drank juice boxes before bed to quiet his mind.

He hit new lows
Like avoiding work by hiding in gym clothes.

The stress got him.
He hit rock bottom.

As the weather warmed,
New thoughts formed.

Walking by friends playing sports,

He felt a strange bulge in his shorts.

It was The F-U-N Mission Statement from months ago!
He reread the words and let go.

He sprinted toward his friends, stood tall,
And booted the kickball.

The ball flew until it was a small, red pea.
In this moment, **he was free.**

Lenny left the cafeteria for his bike seat.
Like normal children, he'd only go there to eat.

Lenny lost the dad and cool kid approval seals,
But he no longer needed their training wheels.

At a rollercoaster park on a school field trip.
Lenny just enjoyed the ride,
Including every twist and dip.

After the ride, his class got lemonade.
At first sip, he rated it second grade.
Not nearly as good as what he once made.

Inspired, he resumed his lemonade pursuit.
He was once again following his passion... fruit.

At the start of the new school year,
Lenny and Noah resumed their lemonade career.

Business was good, and spirits were up.

It was just two boys, one cup.

Lenny's dad was upset,
Uncertain on how much income Lenny would net.

Lenny knew all would be fine.
He valued his love of lemonade
As the bottom line.

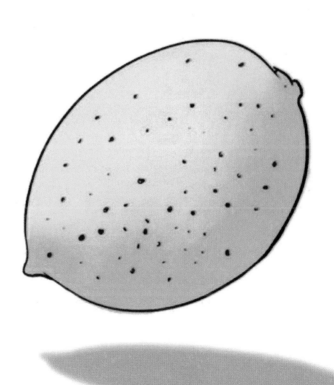

Made in the USA
Las Vegas, NV
24 April 2022

47925972R00040